For Anna, with all my love . . . ~ T. C.
For Harriet and the Scotties! ~ T. W.

Copyright © 2012 by Good Books, Intercourse, PA 17534
International Standard Book Number: 978-1-56148-742-4
Library of Congress Catalog Card Number: 2011031772

Text copyright © Tracey Corderoy 2012
Illustrations copyright © Tim Warnes 2012
Original edition published in English by Little Tiger Press,
an imprint of Magi Publications, London, England, 2012
LTP/1800/0295/1011 • Printed in China

Library of Congress Cataloging-in-Publication Data
Corderoy, Tracey.
Monty and Milli / Tracey Corderoy ; [illustrated by] Tim Warnes.
p. cm.
ISBN 978-1-56148-742-4 (hardcover : alk. paper) [1. Brothers and
sisters--Fiction. 2. Mice--Fiction. 3. Magic tricks--Fiction.]
I. Warnes, Tim, ill. II. Title.
PZ7.C815354Mo 2012
[E]--dc23
2011031772

"Wheeeeeeeeee!"

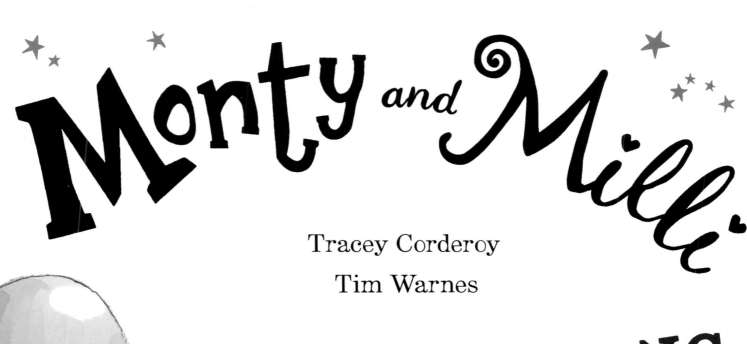

Monty and Milli

Tracey Corderoy

Tim Warnes

The Totally AMAZING Magic Trick

Good Books

Intercourse, PA 17534, 800/762-7171
www.GoodBooks.com

Everything Monty did...

Milli did, too.

CRASH!

When Monty roared, Milli roared.

When Monty painted . . .
so did Milli!

And whenever Monty curled up
with his favorite book...

Read to me, Monty—
pleeeeease?

guess who always
showed up with **hers**?!

"No, Milli," he said,
"it's meant for just **one**…"

ME!

one hat.

She took it pretty
well, considering.

"Actually," piped up Milli, "magicians always shut their eyes."

Monty shut his eyes. "**Kazaam**?" he said. He peeped through his fingers...

...He'd done it!

My BIG BOX MAGIC TRICKS

Totally Amazing Magic Tricks

"Whoopee!" yelled Monty.
"I'm **magic!**"

Hee hee!

But **something** just didn't feel **quite** right...

"Milli!"

cried Monty.

His sister sniffed. "I only wanted to help."
"Well, **don't!**" Monty scowled.

But then Monty remembered—
all the best magicians had helpers…
"Ok," he said. "You can help.
But no taking over."
"**Me**?" squeaked Milli.
"But I **never**
take over…

…EVER!"

Milli **tried** not to take over.

Watch this, Monty...

She tried again and again until...

"Whoops!"

RRRRIPPP!

For the rest of the day Monty practiced his magic **without** Milli's help. He practiced on his tadpole (who didn't complain).

Pick a card— any card...

Then he practiced on his grandma (who did).

Rope tricks
1
2
3

Sometimes things went a little bit wrong, but Monty didn't care!

Being by himself, for once, was fun!

"Monty..." said Dad at snacktime, "where's Milli? Have you seen her?"

Monty checked behind his back. Then around his legs. Milli wasn't in any of her **usual** places. "Nope," he shrugged. "No Milli."

Then he gasped.
"Oh, no! I think I've turned my sister into
a **warty toad!**"

Monty sniffed. "I didn't **mean** it!
I love her really."

"Surprise!"

squealed Milli, shooting out
from under the table.

She gave Monty a **huge** Milli hug.
"You didn't magic me really, **Silly!**" she giggled.

Later, when Monty snuggled into bed,
Milli snuggled in, too. "Monty," she said sleepily,
"you **are** magic, I'm sure."

"Really?" grinned Monty.
"**very** really," Milli
grinned back.

She closed her eyes and he closed his.

"Think of a **huge**, fluffy bunny..." she yawned,
"and I bet you'll magic it up!"

"I wish..." smiled Monty, drifting off to sleep.

The wand slipped from his fingers and...

FWIP!